Where Do Butterflies Go?

Kari McAteer

Illustrated By:
Kenn Yapsangco

Copyright © 2013 by Kari McAteer. 142070-MCAT

ISBN: Softcover   978-1-4931-4908-7
        EBook   978-1-4931-4909-4

All rights reserved. No part of this book may
be reproduced or transmitted in any form or by
any means, electronic or mechanical, including
photocopying, recording, or by any information storage
and retrieval system, without permission in writing from
the copyright owner.

This is a work of fiction. Names, characters,
places and incidents either are the product of the
author's imagination or are used fictitiously, and any
resemblance to any actual persons, living or dead,
events, or locales is entirely coincidental.

Rev. date: 12/12/2013

To order additional copies of this book, contact:
Xlibris LLC
1-888-795-4274
www.Xlibris.com
Orders@Xlibris.com

For Sarah, Alaina, Emily,
Aleeya and Kayla,
with lots of love.
– K. M.

One warm and sunny day, Lacey was playing outside in the backyard, when she noticed something small and wiggly crawling in the garden.

"Look Mommy!" she exclaimed, "It's a caterpillar!" Anxious to see what her daughter had found, Lacey's mother walked from where she had been hanging laundry on the clothes line, over to the edge of the garden. Lacey was crouched down touching the tiny little caterpillar and was closely examining everything about it. "This caterpillar's going to be a monarch butterfly!" she declared to her mother. "What makes you think that honey?" inquired Lacey's mother, rather curiously.

Lacey turned to look at her mother who was now crouched down beside her and remarked, "I read a book about caterpillars at school, and it said that the orange and black striped ones turn into monarch butterflies." Lacey paused for a moment, then added, "Monarch's are the most colourful of all the butterflies!" She watched intently as the little caterpillar inched its way along the bed of the garden, slowly making its way over to a nearby leaf. "Mommy?" asked Lacey, "Once caterpillars turn into butterflies, what happens to them?" she inquired. "What do you mean?" questioned her mother. Without hesitation, Lacey responded. "I mean, where do butterflies go once they have wings to fly away?"

Lacey's mother smiled to herself, impressed by Lacey's keen new interest in butterflies. Promptly she added, "Well honey, I think butterflies go to the place where all butterflies live." Lacey's curiosity was building. "And where's that Mommy?" she inquired. But before Lacey's mother could answer her,

Lacey had suddenly stood up and began to dance and move around. She was holding her arms outwards and was pretending that she was flying like a butterfly. For a moment, Lacey imagined . . ."If I were a butterfly, I would fly away to a warm and sunny place where there's no snow, so I wouldn't get cold and where it doesn't rain, so I wouldn't get wet! It would be a wonderful place!

4

It would be like a big meadow or a beautiful garden, filled with different coloured flowers that I could rest and sit on, when I got tired of flying around!" Lacey's mother looked at Lacey and remarked,

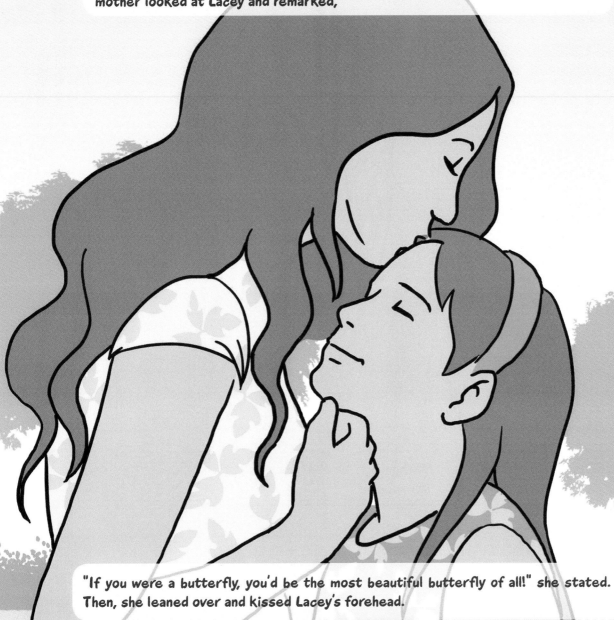

"If you were a butterfly, you'd be the most beautiful butterfly of all!" she stated. Then, she leaned over and kissed Lacey's forehead.

5

Lacey smiled at her mother, as she picked up the bee-striped caterpillar and placed it on the back of her hand. She watched as it gradually moved its way up her arm, tickling her skin as it crawled. "I think this caterpillar is a girl" she proclaimed. "Mommy, can we keep her, PLEASE?!!" she begged. Lacey's mother thought about it for a moment then said, "Ok, but just until she becomes a butterfly, and then we must let her go, alright?" she stated. Lacey nodded in agreement and let out a small squeal of delight. "I think I'll call her Flutter!" she said. Lacey's mother went inside the house to look for a spare jar to put the caterpillar in.

6

Then, her mother carefully poked five small air holes into the top of the lid so that "Flutter" would have enough air to breathe.

Lacey placed the caterpillar inside the jar and watched as it crawled around, quickly becoming accustomed to her new but temporary home. "I think she likes it in there, Mommy," boasted Lacey. "I can't wait to see her change into a monarch!" she proclaimed.

Each day, Lacey watched eagerly as Flutter, the tiny caterpillar, began to change and act differently. She noticed that Flutter had proceeded to hang upside down from one of the twigs she'd placed inside the jar. After awhile, a silky type blanket began to form around Flutter.

A bit perplexed, she took the jar to her mother to show her what she had discovered. "What is that, Mommy?" she asked, as she pointed to the twig inside the jar where Flutter was hanging from. "It's a chrysalis," her mother stated, "Which is a protective shell (kind of like a house) that caterpillars live inside during metamorphosis." Lacey looked a bit confused. "Mommy, what is metamorphosis?" Her mother then clarified, "Metamorphosis is simply the process in which caterpillars (or larvae as they're known) grow and turn into winged adults, or butterflies, as we call them." Lacey looked excited at the thought of watching Flutter turn into a butterfly.

For days and days, she continued to monitor Flutter's progress, in anticipation of the soon-to-be drastic makeover, for the tiny little caterpillar. Then, after about two weeks, it finally happened!

"Mommy, Mommy, come quick, HURRY!" she demanded. Lacey's mother ran to see what all the excitement was about.

"LOOK!" beamed Lacey. Her face was filled with such surprise! "Flutter now has wings!" she shouted. "Wow!" she cheered.

Lacey's mother picked up the jar and looked inside of it. She saw the torn chrysalis hanging from the small twig, where the once small caterpillar had been growing and changing inside of it. She marvelled at the sight of the now beautiful, orange and black monarch butterfly that was twirling and fluttering all around the jar. "It's time," her mother said, then she handed Lacey the jar. "Do you think that Flutter will come back to visit us Mommy?" She asked wishfully. "I certainly hope so," said her mother. Lacey grinned. As much as she wanted to keep Flutter, Lacey knew that her mother was right, and that she had to set the butterfly free.

Lacey untwisted the lid of the jar and Flutter flew out! For a moment or two, she floated all around Lacey and her mother, twirling and flying so gently and gracefully.

"Good bye Flutter" sighed Lacey sadly. She watched as her beautiful new butterfly, flew away. Before long, Flutter had quickly faded away and out of their sight.

"Mommy?" asked Lacey, "Do you think she'll be happy there?" pondered Lacey. "Happy where?" said her mother. "You know . . . the place where butterflies go." Lacey's mother nodded. "Yes of course she will" she stated. "She will probably think about you while she's enjoying her new and happy life as a monarch butterfly." Lacey agreed. "Yeah, she probably will."

Despite the fact that Lacey missed her, she knew deep down that Flutter was where she wanted to be . . . migrating to somewhere warm and dry; in a paradise of vibrant colours, filled with delightful fragrances and flowers; a place that's as beautiful as she turned out to be. Flutter was now finally free and in the place she really loved . . . the place where butterflies go!

CPSIA information can be obtained
at www.ICGtesting.com
Printed in the USA
LVIC06n2358010714
392592LV00003B/25

9781493149087